THE ONE AND ONLY
SHREK!

◈ ◈ ◈ ◈ ◈ ◈ ◈

PLUS 5 OTHER STORIES

THE ONE AND ONLY
SHREK!
PLUS 5 OTHER STORIES

● ● ● ● ● ●

WILLIAM · STEIG

SQUARE
FISH

Farrar, Straus and Giroux
New York

The One and Only SHREK! Plus 5 Other Stories
Introduction copyright © 2007 by Eric Carle
All rights reserved
Distributed in Canada by H. B. Fenn and Company, Ltd.
Square Fish
A Division of Holtzbrinck Publishers
175 Fifth Avenue, New York, NY 10010
Printed and bound in the United States of America
Designed by Barbara Grzeslo and Polly Kanevsky
First Square Fish Edition: 2007
1   3   5   7   9   10   8   6   4   2

Library of Congress Cataloging-in-Publication Data
Steig, William, 1907–2003.
    The one and only Shrek! : plus 5 other stories / William Steig.— 1st Square Fish ed.
        v.   cm.
    Contents: Shrek! — The amazing bone — Brave Irene — Spinky sulks — Doctor De Soto — Caleb & Kate.
    ISBN-13: 978-0-312-36713-8
    ISBN-10: 0-312-36713-9
    1. Children's stories, American.   I. Title.

PZ7.S8177 On 2007
[Fic]—dc22

2006029451

These books were originally published by Farrar, Straus and Giroux, LLC

Original copyrights and dedications:
SHREK! by William Steig
Copyright © 1990 by William Steig
To Emma, Jonathan, Alicia, Will, Kate, Jonas, and Carol Regnier

The Amazing Bone by William Steig
Copyright © 1976 by William Steig
To Maggie, Melinda, Francesca, and Nika

Brave Irene by William Steig
Copyright © 1986 by William Steig
For Jeanne

Spinky Sulks by William Steig
Copyright © 1988 by William Steig
To Jonathan, Alicia, Sido, Estelle, Jonas, Kyle, and Serena

Doctor De Soto by William Steig
Copyright © 1982 by William Steig
To Delia, Sidonie, Sylvain, Estelle, Kyle, Molly, Reid, Tina, Serena, Zachary, and Zoe

Caleb & Kate by William Steig
Copyright © 1977 by William Steig
To Delia, Nika, Abigail, and Francesca

Contents

Introduction

It was an honor for the Eric Carle Museum of Picture Book Art to host an exhibition of William Steig's artwork and Jeanne Steig's sculpture in 2004. And I feel equally honored now to write a few words about William Steig, this luminary figure and creative genius who has made such an important contribution to the world of picture books.

I had been an admirer of William Steig's cartoons in *The New Yorker* before he created his picture books. And it did not take me long to treasure these new works: their humor and soulfulness, their energetic language and imaginative twists and turns, and the range and depth of their characters' emotions. I love how when characters like Caleb and Kate, who come so close to never seeing one another again, are reunited, one cannot help but feel one's own heart rise up.

But most of all, I love the free feeling in the pictures and stories of William Steig. As Jane Bayard Curley wrote in her essay "A Life of Creative Energy," "His imagination simply flowed through the pen and onto the page." No true artist or creative person would disagree: this freedom, this flow, is what we all strive for.

All of the works in this wonderful collection—*SHREK!*, *The Amazing Bone*, *Brave Irene*, *Spinky Sulks*, *Doctor De Soto*, and *Caleb & Kate*—tell stories that will continue to be enjoyed by readers of all ages for as long as children's books are read.

—Eric Carle

His mother was ugly and his father was ugly, but Shrek was uglier than
the two of them put together. By the time he toddled, Shrek could spit
flame a full ninety-nine yards and vent smoke from either ear. With just a
look he cowed the reptiles in the swamp. Any snake dumb enough to bite
him instantly got convulsions and died.

One day Shrek's parents hissed things over and decided it was about time their little darling was out in the world doing his share of damage. So they kicked him goodbye and Shrek left the black hole in which he'd been hatched.

Shrek went slogging along the road, giving off his awful fumes. It delighted him to see the flowers bend aside and the trees lean away to let him go by.

In a shady copse, he came across a witch. She was busy boiling bats in turpentine and turtle juice, and as she stirred, she crooned:

> *"This is the way I cook my bats,*
> *Stir my bats, taste my bats,*
> *Season my bats in the morning;*
> *Stew and brew and chew my bats,*
> *Diddle and fiddle and faddle my bats,*
> *Early in the morning."*

"What a lovely stench!" Shrek cackled. The witch specialized in horrors, but one single look at Shrek made her woozy.

When she recovered her senses, Shrek said, "Tell my fortune, madam, and I'll let you have a few of my rare lice."

"Splendid!" crowed the witch. "Here's your fortune.

"Otchky-potchky, itchky-pitch,
Pay attention to this witch.
A donkey takes you to a knight—
Him you conquer in a fight.
Then you wed a princess who
Is even uglier than you.
Ha ha ha and cockadoodle,
The magic words are 'Apple Strudel.'"

"A princess!" **Shrek cried.** "I'm on my way!"

Soon he came upon a peasant singing and scything. "You there, varlet," said Shrek. "Why so blithe?"

The peasant mumbled this reply:

"I'm happy scything in the rye,
I never stop to wonder why.
I'll hone and scythe until I die.
But now I'm busy. So goodbye."

"Yokel," Shrek snapped. "What have you in that pouch of yours?"

"Just some cold pheasant."

"Pheasant, peasant? What a pleasant present!"

The last thing the peasant saw before he fainted was Shrek's glare warming up his dinner. Shrek ate and moved on.

Wherever Shrek went, every living creature fled. How it tickled him to be so repulsive!

Fat raindrops began sizzling on Shrek's hot knob.

"Did you ever see somebody so disgusting?" said Lightning to Thunder.

"Never," Thunder growled. "Let's give him the works."

Lightning fired his fiercest bolt straight at Shrek's head. Shrek just gobbled it, belched some smoke, and grinned. Lightning, Thunder, and Rain departed.

In high spirits, Shrek stalked on. At the edge of a woods, he found this warning nailed to a tree:

> *Harken, stranger.*
> *Shun the danger!*
> *If you plan to stay the same,*
> *You'd best go back from whence you came.*

Shrek, of course, swaggered right past.

And sure enough, a little way into the woods, a whopper of a dragon barred his path. Shrek smiled and bowed. The dragon slammed him to the ground, but Shrek just lay there. He was amused.

The irascible dragon was preparing to separate Shrek from his noggin.
But Shrek got him between the eyes with a putrid blue flame.
The poor dragon thudded over, unconscious for the day.

An hour later, Shrek himself was unconscious. He had fallen asleep along the way. He dreamed he was in a field of flowers where children frolicked and birds warbled. Some of the children kept hugging and kissing him, and there was nothing he could do to make them stop.

He woke up in a daze, babbling like a baby: "It was only a bad dream . . . a horrible dream!"

Shrek wandered on. He was wondering if he'd ever meet his princess, when he saw a donkey grazing. Was this the donkey the witch had foretold? Shrek hurried over and tried the magic words: "Apple Strudel!"

The donkey raised his sleepy eyes and brayed:

> *"I gaze in the green*
> *As I graze in the green,*
> *Seeking out the clover.*
> *I laze and spend my days in the green,*
> *A chewing, chomping rover."*

"You jabbering jackass!" Shrek screamed. "Aren't you supposed to take me somewhere?"

"I am. To the nutty knight. Who guards the entrance. To the crazy castle. Where the repulsive princess. Waits."

"Then take!" Shrek shrieked, and he hopped onto the donkey's back.

They soon came to a drawbridge where a suit of armor stood. Shrek knocked on the breastplate and demanded: "Who dwells inside this armor, and also in yonder castle?"

"In here a fearless knight, in there a well-born fright" was the answer.

"It's my princess!" said Shrek. "The one I'm to wed!"

"Over my dead body!" roared the fearless knight.

"Over your dead body," Shrek agreed.

"Not so brave, thou churlish knave!" countered the knight.

"Do me the honor to step aside, so Shrek can go to meet his bride," Shrek commanded.

"Magician's mercury, plumber's lead, I smite your stupid, scabby head." And the knight smote.

Shrek popped his eyes, opened his trap, and bellowed a blast of fire.
The knight, red-hot, dove into the stagnant moat.

With a nasty snort of triumph, Shrek crossed the bridge and marched into the castle. And there, for the first time ever, he found out what fear was.

All around him were hundreds of hideous creatures. He was so appalled he could barely manage to spit a bit of flame. All those horrid others spat back. He started to run; they all ran. He lashed out at the nearest one, but what he struck was glass.

Shrek was in the Hall of Mirrors! "They're all me!" he yodeled. "ALL ME!" He faced himself, full of rabid self-esteem, happier than ever to be exactly what he was.

He strode on in and his fat lips fell open. There before him was the most stunningly ugly princess on the surface of the planet.

"Apple Strudel," Shrek sighed.

"Cockadoodoodle," cooed the princess.

Said Shrek: "Your horny warts, your rosy wens,
               Like slimy bogs and fusty fens,
               Thrill me."

Said the princess: "Your lumpy nose, your pointy head,
                      Your wicked eyes, so livid red,
                      Just kill me."

Said Shrek: "Oh, ghastly you,   "I could go on,
              With lips of blue,   I know you know
              Your ruddy eyes   The reason why
              With carmine sties   I love you so—
              Enchant me.   You're ugh-ly!"

Said the princess: "Your nose is so hairy,
                     Oh, let us not tarry,
                     Your look is so scary,
                     I think we should marry."

Shrek snapped at her nose. She nipped at his ear. They clawed their way into each other's arms. Like fire and smoke, these two belonged together.

So they got hitched as soon as possible. And they lived horribly ever after, scaring the socks off all who fell afoul of them.

THE
AMAZING
BONE

It was a brilliant day, and instead of going straight home from school, Pearl dawdled. She watched the grownups in town at their grownup work, things she might someday be doing.

She saw the street cleaners sweeping the streets and she looked in at the bakery on Parsnip Lane and saw the bakers taking hot loaves of pumpernickel out of the oven and powdering crullers with sugar dust.

On Cobble Road she stopped at Maltby's barn and stood gawking as
the old gaffers pitched their ringing horseshoes and spat tobacco juice.

Later she sat on the ground in the forest between school and home, and spring was so bright and beautiful, the warm air touched her so tenderly, she could almost feel herself changing into a flower. Her light dress felt like petals.

"I love everything," she heard herself say.

"So do I," a voice answered.

Pearl straightened up and looked around. No one was there. "Where are you?" she asked.

"Look down," came the answer. Pearl looked down. "I'm the bone in the violets near the tree by the rock on your right."

Pearl stared at a small bone. "You talk?" she murmured.

"In any language," said the bone. "¿Habla español? Rezumiesh

popolsku? Sprechen sie Deutsch? And I can imitate any sound there is."
The bone made the sounds of a trumpet calling soldiers to arms. Then it
sounded like wind blowing, then like pattering rain. Then it snored, then
sneezed.

Pearl couldn't believe what she was hearing. "You're a bone," she said.
"How come you can sneeze?"

"I don't know," the bone replied. "I didn't make the world."

"May I take you home with me, wonderful bone?" Pearl asked.

"You certainly may," said the bone. "I've been alone a long time. A year ago, come August, I fell out of a witch's basket. I could have yelled after her as she walked on, but I didn't want to be her bone any longer. She ate snails cooked in garlic at every meal and was always complaining about her rheumatism and asking nosy questions. I'd be happier with someone young and lively like you."

Pearl picked the bone up and gently put it in her purse. She left the purse open, so they could continue their talk, and started home, forgetting her schoolbooks on the grass. She was eager to show this bone to her

parents, and she could guess what would happen when she did. She would tell about the talking bone, her mother would say "You're only imagining it," her father would agree, and then the bone would flabbergast them both by talking.

The spring green sparkled in the spring light. Tree toads were trilling. "It's the kind of wonderful day," said Pearl, "when wonderful things happen—like my finding you."

"Like *my* finding *you*!" the bone answered. And it began to whistle a walking tune that made the going very pleasant.

But not for long. Who should rush out from in back of a boulder and spoil everything but three highway robbers with pistols and daggers. Pearl couldn't tell what breed of animal they were, because they wore cloaks and Halloween masks, but they were fierce and spoke in chilling voices.

"Hand over the purse!" one commanded. Pearl would have gladly surrendered the purse, just to be rid of them, but not with the bone in it.

"You can't have my purse," she said, surprised at her own boldness.
"What's in it?" said another robber, pointing his gun at Pearl's head.

"I'm in it!" the bone growled. And it began to hiss like a snake and roar like a lion.

The robbers didn't wait around to hear the rest, in case there was any more. They fled so fast you couldn't tell which way they'd gone. It made Pearl laugh. The bone, too.

They continued on their way, joking about what had just happened and chatting about this and that. But it wasn't long before a fox stepped forth from behind a tree and barred their path. He wore a sprig of lilac in his lapel, he carried a cane, and he was grinning so the whole world could see his sharp white teeth.

"Hold everything," he said. Pearl froze. "You're exactly what I've been longing for," he went on. "Young, plump, and tender. You will be my main course at dinner tonight." And he seized Pearl in a tight embrace.

"Unhand her, you villain," the bone screamed, "or I'll bite your ears off!"

"Who is that speaking?" asked the surprised fox.

"A ravenous crocodile who dotes on fresh fox chops, that's who!" answered the bone.

The wily fox was not as easily duped as the robbers. He saw no dangerous crocodile. He peered into Pearl's purse, where the sounds seemed to be coming from, and pulled out the bone. "As I live and flourish!" he exclaimed. "A talking bone. I've always wanted to own something of this sort." And he put the bone in his pocket, where it roared and ranted to no avail.

Pushing Pearl along, the fox set out for his hideaway. Pearl's sobs were so pitiful the fox couldn't help feeling a little sorry for her, but he was determined she would be his dinner.

"Please, Mr. Fox," Pearl whimpered, "may I have my bone back, at least until I have to die?"

"Oh, all right," said the fox, disgusted with himself for being so softhearted, and he handed her the bone, which she put back in her purse.

"You must let this beautiful young creature go on living," the bone yelled. "Have you no shame, sir!"

The fox laughed. "Why should I be ashamed? I can't help being the way I am. I didn't make the world."

The bone commenced to revile the fox. "You coward!" it sneered. "You worm, you odoriferous wretch!"

These expletives were annoying. "Shut up, or I'll eat you," the fox snarled. "It would be amusing to gnaw on a bone that talks . . . and screams with pain."

The bone kept quiet the rest of the way, and so did Pearl.

When they arrived at the fox's hideaway, he shoved Pearl, with her bone, into an empty room and locked the door. Pearl sat on the floor and stared at the walls.

"I know how you feel," the bone whispered.

"I'm only just beginning to live," Pearl whispered back. "I don't want it to end."

"I know," said the bone.

"Isn't there something we can do?" Pearl asked.

"I wish I could think of something," said the bone, "but I can't. I feel miserable."

"What's *that*?" Pearl asked. She'd heard some sounds from the kitchen.

"He's sharpening a knife," the bone whispered.

"Oh, my goodness!" Pearl sobbed. "And what's *that*?"

"Sounds like wood being put into a stove," answered the bone.

"I hope it won't all take too long," said Pearl. She could smell vinegar and oil. The fox was preparing a salad to go with his meal. Pearl hugged the bone to her breast. "Bone, say something to comfort me."

"You are very dear to me," said the bone.

"Oh, how dear you are to me!" Pearl replied. She could hear a key in the lock and was unable to get another word out of her throat or turn her eyes toward the door.

"Be brave," the bone whispered. Pearl could only tremble.

She was dragged into the kitchen, where she could see flames in the open stove.

"I regret having to do this to you," sighed the fox. "It's nothing personal."

"*Yibbam!*" said the bone suddenly, without knowing why he said it.

"What was that?" said the fox, standing stock-still.

"Yibbam sibibble!" the bone intoned. "Jibrakken sibibble digray!" And something quite unexpected took place. The fox grew several inches shorter.

"Alabam chinook beboppit gebozzle!" the bone continued, and miraculously the fox was the size of a rabbit. No one could believe what was happening, not Pearl, not the fox, not even the bone, whose words were making it happen.

"Adoonis ishgoolak keebokkin yibapp!" it went on. The fox, clothes and all, was now the size of a mouse.

"Scrabboonit!" the bone ordered, and the mouse—that is, the minuscule fox—scurried away and into a hole.

"I didn't know you could do magic!" Pearl breathlessly exclaimed.

"Neither did I," said the bone.

"Well, what made you say those words?"

"I wish I knew," the bone said. "They just came to me, I *had* to say them. I must have picked them up somehow, hanging around with that witch."

"You're an amazing bone," said Pearl, "and this is a day I won't ever forget!"

It was dark when they reached Pearl's house. The moment the door swung open she was in her mother's arms, and right after that in her father's.

"Where on earth have you been?" they both wanted to know. "We were frazzled with worry."

Pearl didn't know what to say first. She held up the bone. "This bone," she said, "can talk!" And just as she had expected, her mother said, "A talking bone? Why, Pearl, it's only your imagination." And her father said something similar. And also as Pearl had expected, the bone astonished them both by remarking, "You have an exceptional daughter."

Before her parents had a chance to get over their shock, Pearl began telling the story of her day's adventure, and the bone helped out. It was all too much for Pearl's parents. Until they got used to it.

The bone stayed on and became part of the family. It was given an honored place in a silver tray on the mantelpiece. Pearl always took it to bed when she retired, and the two chatterboxes whispered together until late in the night. Sometimes the bone put Pearl to sleep by singing, or by imitating soft harp music.

Anyone who happened to be alone in the house always had the bone to converse with. And they all had music whenever they wanted it, and sometimes even when they didn't.

BRAVE
IRENE

Mrs. Bobbin, the dressmaker, was tired and had a bad headache, but she still managed to sew the last stitches in the gown she was making.

"It's the most beautiful dress in the whole world!" said her daughter, Irene. "The duchess will love it."

"It *is* nice," her mother admitted. "But, dumpling, it's for tonight's ball, and I don't have the strength to bring it. I feel sick."

"Poor Mama," said Irene. "I can get it there!"

"No, cupcake, I can't let you," said Mrs. Bobbin. "Such a huge package, and it's such a long way to the palace. Besides, it's starting to snow."

"But I *love* snow," Irene insisted. She coaxed her mother into bed, covered her with two quilts, and added a blanket for her feet. Then she fixed her some tea with lemon and honey and put more wood in the stove.

With great care, Irene took the splendid gown down from the dummy and packed it in a big box with plenty of tissue paper.

"Dress warmly, pudding," her mother called in a weak voice, "and don't forget to button up. It's cold out there, and windy."

Irene put on her fleece-lined boots, her red hat and muffler, her heavy coat, and her mittens. She kissed her mother's hot forehead six times, then once again, made sure she was tucked in snugly, and slipped out with the big box, shutting the door firmly behind her.

It really was cold outside, very cold. The wind whirled the falling snowflakes about, this way, that way, and into Irene's squinting face. She set out on the uphill path to Farmer Bennett's sheep pasture.

By the time she got there, the snow was up to her ankles and the wind was worse. It hurried her along and made her stumble. Irene resented this; the box was problem enough. "Easy does it!" she cautioned the wind, leaning back hard against it.

By the middle of the pasture, the flakes were falling thicker. Now the wind drove Irene along so rudely she had to hop, skip, and go helter-skeltering over the knobby ground. Cold snow sifted into her boots and chilled her feet. She pushed out her lip and hurried on. This was an important errand.

When she reached Apple Road, the wind decided to put on a show. It ripped branches from trees and flung them about, swept up and scattered the fallen snow, got in front of Irene to keep her from moving ahead. Irene turned around and pressed on backwards.

"Go home!" the wind squalled. "Irene . . . go hoooooome . . ."

"I will do no such thing," she snapped. "No such thing, you wicked wind!"

"Go ho–o–ome," the wind yodeled. "GO HO—WO—WOME," it shrieked, "or else." For a short second, Irene wondered if she shouldn't heed the wind's warning. But no! *The gown had to get to the duchess!*

The wind wrestled her for the package—walloped it, twisted it, shook it, snatched at it. But Irene wouldn't yield. "It's my mother's work!" she screamed.

Then—oh, woe!—the box was wrenched from her mittened grasp and sent bumbling along in the snow. Irene went after it.

She pounced and took hold, but the ill-tempered wind ripped the box open. The ball gown flounced out and went waltzing through the powdered air with tissue-paper attendants.

Irene clung to the empty box and watched the beautiful gown disappear.

How could anything so terribly wrong be allowed to happen? Tears froze on her lashes. Her dear mother's hard work, all those days of measuring, cutting, pinning, stitching . . . for *this*? And the poor duchess! Irene decided she would have to trudge on with just the box and explain everything in person.

She went shuffling through the snow. Would her mother understand, she wondered, that it was the wind's fault, not hers? Would the duchess be angry? The wind was howling like a wild animal.

Suddenly Irene stepped in a hole and fell over with a twisted ankle. She blamed it on the wind. "Keep quiet!" she scolded. "You've done enough damage already. You've spoiled everything! *Everything!*" The wind swallowed up her words.

She sat in the snow in great pain, afraid she wouldn't be able to go on. But she managed to get to her feet and start moving. It hurt. Home, where she longed to be, where she and her mother could be warm together, was far behind. It's got to be closer to the palace, she thought. But where any place was in all this snow, she couldn't be sure.

She plowed on, dragging furrows with her sore foot. The short winter day was almost done.

Am I still going the right way, she wondered. There was no one around to advise her. Whoever else there was in this snow-covered world was far, far away, and safe indoors—even the animals in their burrows. She went plodding on.

Soon night took over. She knew in the dark that the muffled snow was still falling—she could feel it. She was cold and alone in the middle of nowhere. Irene was lost.

She had to keep moving. She was hoping she'd come to a house, any house at all, and be taken in. She badly needed to be in someone's arms. The snow was above her knees now. She shoved her way through it, clutching the empty box.

She was asking how long a small person could keep this struggle up, when she realized it was getting lighter. There was a soft glow coming from somewhere below her.

She waded toward this glow, and soon was gazing down a long slope at a brightly lit mansion. It had to be the palace!

Irene pushed forward with all her strength and—*sloosh! thwump!*—
she plunged downward and was buried. She had fallen off a little cliff.
Only her hat and the box in her hands stuck out above the snow.

Even if she could call for help, no one would hear her. Her body
shook. Her teeth chattered. Why not freeze to death, she thought, and let
all these troubles end. Why not? She was already buried.

And never see her mother's face again? Her good mother who smelled like fresh-baked bread? In an explosion of fury, she flung her body about to free herself and was finally able to climb up on her knees and look around.

How to get down to that glittering palace? As soon as she raised the question, she had the answer.

She laid the box down and climbed aboard. But it pressed into the snow and stuck. She tried again, and this time, instead of climbing on, she leaped. The box shot forward, like a sled.

The wind raced after Irene but couldn't keep up. In a moment she would be with people again, inside where it was warm. The sled slowed and jerked to a stop on paving stones.

The time had come to break the bad news to the duchess. With the empty box clasped to her chest, Irene strode nervously toward the palace.

But then her feet stopped moving and her mouth fell open. She stared. Maybe this was impossible, yet there it was, a little way off and over to the right, hugging the trunk of a tree—the beautiful ball gown! The wind was holding it there.

"Mama!" Irene shouted. "Mama, I found it!"

She managed somehow, despite the wind's meddling, to get the gown off the tree and back in its box. And in another moment she was at the door of the palace. She knocked twice with the big brass knocker. The door opened and she burst in.

She was welcomed by cheering servants and a delirious duchess. They couldn't believe she had come over the mountain in such a storm, all by herself. She had to tell the whole story, every detail. And she did.

Then she asked to be taken right back to her sick mother. But it was out of the question, they said; the road that ran around the mountain wouldn't be cleared till morning.

"Don't fret, child," said the duchess. "Your mother is surely sleeping now. We'll get you there first thing tomorrow."

Irene was given a good dinner as she sat by the fire, the moisture steaming off her clothes. The duchess, meanwhile, got into her freshly ironed gown before the guests began arriving in their sleighs.

What a wonderful ball it was! The duchess in her new gown was like
a bright star in the sky. Irene in her ordinary dress was radiant. She was

swept up into dances by handsome aristocrats, who kept her feet off the floor to spare her ankle. Her mother would enjoy hearing all about it.

Early the next morning, when snow had long since ceased falling, Mrs. Bobbin woke from a good night's sleep feeling much improved. She hurried about and got a fire going in the cold stove. Then she went to look in on Irene.

But Irene's bed was empty! She ran to the window and gazed at the white landscape. No one out there. Snow powder fell from the branch of a tree.

"Where is my child?" Mrs. Bobbin cried. She whipped on her coat to go out and find her.

When she pulled the door open, a wall of drift faced her. But peering over it, she could see a horse-drawn sleigh hastening up the path. And seated on the sleigh, between two large footmen, was Irene herself, asleep but smiling.

Would you like to hear the rest?

Well, there was a bearded doctor in the back of the sleigh. And the duchess had sent Irene's mother a ginger cake with white icing, some oranges and a pineapple, and spice candy of many flavors, along with a note saying how much she cherished her gown, and what a brave and loving person Irene was.

Which, of course, Mrs. Bobbin knew. Better than the duchess.

SPINKY SULKS

Spinky came charging out of the house and flung himself on the grass. He couldn't even see the dandelions he was staring at, he was so upset. His stupid family! They were supposed to love him, but the heck they did. Not even his mother.

In a while his sister, Willamina, came out and said, "I'm sorry I called you Stinky, Spinky." Spinky didn't answer.

"Spinkalink," she said. "I apologize!" Spinky still didn't answer, so she went back inside. "*Now* she apologizes," he muttered.

A little later Spinky's brother, Hitch, appeared and touched him with a finger. Spinky shook it off. "You were posilutely right!" Hitch said. "I looked it up. Philadelphia *is* the capital of Belgium."

Spinky turned his back. His brother's slimy voice was more than he could bear.

"Spinks, it's lunchtime," said Hitch. "Mama wants you in the house."

Instead of answering, Spinky went and climbed the big tree.

His parents were watching from the window. "Poor kid, he's so sensitive," said his mother. "I better go talk to him, Harry."

"Ruby, don't," his father said. "He needs to simmer down. He's got no reason to sulk."

When it started getting dark, Spinky's mother came outside. She kissed him over and over, and told him she loved him with all her heart, ever since the minute he was born. And even before that.

Then she covered him with a blanket and kissed him again—and it was no fake kiss. But Spinky lay there like a stone. He wasn't interested in kisses that came too late.

The next morning, when Spinky's father left for work, Spinky was nowhere in sight.

Two seconds later he was in back of the house kicking a kerosene can. "Some father!" he snorted.

At noon Spinky's mother brought him a tray. Spinky didn't even look at her. "All of a sudden they're being nice!" he thought.

When she came back, the tomato soup and the asparagus were still there, but the crullers and the grapes were gone.

Hitch and Willamina kept finding Spinky in different places.

They'd try to pry a word out of him, or they'd just pass him by.

Hitch got down on his ugly knees once and begged to be forgiven for anything he had ever done that Spinky took exception to. This only made Spinky loathe him all the more.

Spinky's mother sat with him and held his hand, but his arm hung down like a noodle.

Willamina picked some daisies and stuck them in the hammock. Spinky threw them out.

Around four o'clock, a circus parade came marching by. "Look, Spinky," his mother cried. "Clowns! Elephants!" But he wouldn't even glance in that direction.

What a family! First they ruin his life, then they expect him to watch a parade.

Spinky's best buddies, Smudge and Iggie, came to visit. Smudge
crawled into the hammock and whispered goofy things in Spinky's ear.
Spinky kicked him out.

Smudge and Iggie tried swinging him. Spinky usually liked that, but not now. He wrapped himself up in the hammock and disappeared, so his friends took off.

That evening Spinky's father gave him a long lecture. He said even though Spinky was wrong to sulk like a baby, everyone still loved him anyway. In fact, maybe he didn't realize it, but he was one of the most popular of the three children.

Spinky had to cover his ears to avoid listening to this malarky. No one seemed to understand that he was a person with his own private thoughts and feelings, which they couldn't begin to appreciate. The world was against him, so he was against the world, and that included all living things—except, of course, the animals.

Spinky's family was worried. They couldn't stand to see him feeling so wretched. That night they had a conference, and Spinky's father made a couple of phone calls.

The next day was a holiday. The sun was radiant, the birds were happy. Spinky couldn't care less. He lay in his hammock like a pile of laundry.

His favorite grandma just happened to stop by with some of his favorite candy. She gave him a big fat hug, but Spinky went limp in her arms.

After all, she still belonged to the human race, for which he no longer had any use.

Just then a circus clown happened to come prancing across the lawn with a sign saying: WE LOVE YOU, SPINKY. The clown winked, reached into Spinky's pocket, and pulled out a triple-dip ice-cream cone (pistachio, banana, and chocolate chip).

Spinky had to laugh. But then he saw his father smirking—and got the picture. The clown had been *hired* to cheer him up. Well, it wouldn't work!

All day long, everybody was as sweet and considerate as they could possibly be. When it started to rain, Spinky's mother covered him with a tarpaulin and his father set up the beach umbrella.

Hitch and Willamina served him cake and sandwiches. Still, Spinky couldn't give in, though he was beginning to consider it.

Maybe these people didn't know how to behave, but at least they were trying. Was it their fault they couldn't do better? He wasn't mad anymore, but he still had his pride. After all his suffering, how could he just turn around and act lovey-dovey? That wasn't his way.

Spinky lay awake wondering how to give in and still keep his self-respect. He decided he would take them by surprise.

Before dawn, he stole into the house and tiptoed about, very busy with secret business.

In the morning, the whole family drifted down to the dining room in a dreary mood. Laid out before them was a splendiferous feast, and there stood a garish clown, inviting them to join him.

Of course, they knew who it was. They laughed so hard it was a long time before they could stop.

After that, Spinky's family was much more careful about his feelings.

Too bad they couldn't keep it up forever.

DOCTOR DE SOTO

Doctor De Soto, the dentist, did very good work, so he had no end of patients. Those close to his own size—moles, chipmunks, et cetera—sat in the regular dentist's chair.

Larger animals sat on the floor, while Doctor De Soto stood on a ladder.

For extra-large animals, he had a special room. There Doctor De Soto was hoisted up to the patient's mouth by his assistant, who also happened to be his wife.

Doctor De Soto was especially popular with the big animals. He was able to work inside their mouths, wearing rubbers to keep his feet dry; and his fingers were so delicate, and his drill so dainty, they could hardly feel any pain.

Being a mouse, he refused to treat animals dangerous to mice, and it said so on his sign. When the doorbell rang, he and his wife would look out the window. They wouldn't admit even the most timid-looking cat.

One day, when they looked out, they saw a well-dressed fox with a flannel bandage around his jaw.

"I cannot treat you, sir!" Doctor De Soto shouted. "Sir! Haven't you read my sign?"

"Please!" the fox wailed. "Have mercy, I'm suffering!" And he wept so bitterly it was pitiful to see.

"Just a moment," said Doctor De Soto. "That poor fox," he whispered to his wife. "What shall we do?"

"Let's risk it," said Mrs. De Soto. She pressed the buzzer and let the fox in.

He was up the stairs in a flash. "Bless your little hearts," he cried, falling to his knees. "I beg you, *do* something! My tooth is killing me."

"Sit on the floor, sir," said Doctor De Soto, "and remove the bandage, please."

Doctor De Soto climbed up the ladder and bravely entered the fox's mouth. "Ooo-wow!" he gasped. The fox had a rotten bicuspid and unusually bad breath.

"This tooth will have to come out," Doctor De Soto announced. "But we can make you a new one."

"Just stop the pain," whimpered the fox, wiping some tears away.

Despite his misery, he realized he had a tasty little morsel in his mouth, and his jaw began to quiver. "Keep open!" yelled Doctor De Soto. "Wide open!" yelled his wife.

"I'm giving you gas now," said Doctor De Soto. "You won't feel a thing when I yank that tooth."

Soon the fox was in dreamland. "M-m-m, yummy," he mumbled. "How I love them raw . . . with just a pinch of salt, and a . . . dry . . . white wine."

They could guess what he was dreaming about. Mrs. De Soto handed her husband a pole to keep the fox's mouth open.

Doctor De Soto fastened his extractor to the bad tooth. Then he and his wife began turning the winch. Finally, with a sucking sound, the tooth popped out and hung swaying in the air.

"I'm bleeding!" the fox yelped when he came to.

Doctor De Soto ran up the ladder and stuffed some gauze in the hole. "The worst is over," he said. "I'll have your new tooth ready tomorrow. Be here at eleven sharp."

The fox, still woozy, said goodbye and left. On his way home, he wondered if it would be shabby of him to eat the De Sotos when the job was done.

After office hours, Mrs. De Soto molded a tooth of pure gold and polished it. "Raw with salt, indeed," muttered Doctor De Soto. "How foolish to trust a fox!"

"He didn't know what he was saying," said Mrs. De Soto. "Why should he harm us? We're helping him."

"Because he's a fox!" said Doctor De Soto. "They're wicked, wicked creatures."

That night the De Sotos lay awake worrying. "Should we let him in tomorrow?" Mrs. De Soto wondered.

"Once I start a job," said the dentist firmly, "I finish it. My father was the same way."

"But we must do something to protect ourselves," said his wife. They talked and talked until they formed a plan. "I think it will work," said Doctor De Soto. A minute later he was snoring.

The next morning, promptly at eleven, a very cheerful fox turned up.
He was feeling not a particle of pain.

When Doctor De Soto got into his mouth, he snapped it shut for a moment, then opened wide and laughed. "Just a joke!" he chortled.

"Be serious," said the dentist sharply. "We have work to do." His wife was lugging the heavy tooth up the ladder.

"Oh, I love it!" exclaimed the fox. "It's just beautiful."

Doctor De Soto set the gold tooth in its socket and hooked it up to the teeth on both sides.

The fox caressed the new tooth with his tongue. "My, it feels good," he thought. "I really shouldn't eat them. On the other hand, how can I resist?"

"We're not finished," said Doctor De Soto, holding up a large jug. "I have here a remarkable preparation developed only recently by my wife and me. With just one application, you can be rid of toothaches forever. How would you like to be the first one to receive this unique treatment?"

"I certainly would!" the fox declared. "I'd be honored." He hated any kind of personal pain.

"You will never have to see us again," said Doctor De Soto.

"*No one* will see you again," said the fox to himself. He had definitely made up his mind to eat them—with the help of his brand-new tooth.

Doctor De Soto stepped into the fox's mouth with a bucket of secret formula and proceeded to paint each tooth. He hummed as he worked. Mrs. De Soto stood by on the ladder, pointing out spots he had missed. The fox looked very happy.

When the dentist was done, he stepped out. "Now close your jaws tight," he said, "and keep them closed for a full minute." The fox did as he was told. Then he tried to open his mouth—but his teeth were stuck together!

"Ah, excuse me, I should have mentioned," said Doctor De Soto, "you won't be able to open your mouth for a day or two. The secret formula must first permeate the dentine. But don't worry. No pain ever again!"

The fox was stunned. He stared at Doctor De Soto, then at his wife. They smiled, and waited. All he could do was say, "Frank oo berry mush" through his clenched teeth, and get up and leave. He tried to do so with dignity.

Then he stumbled down the stairs in a daze.

Doctor De Soto and his assistant had outfoxed the fox. They kissed each other and took the rest of the day off.

CALEB & KATE

Caleb the carpenter and Kate the weaver loved each other, but not every single minute. Once in a while they'd differ about this or that and wind up in such a fierce quarrel you'd never believe they were husband and wife.

During one of those crazy quarrels, Caleb got so angry he slammed out of the house hating his wife from top to bottom; and she, for her part, screamed after him the most odious insults that came to her mouth.

Caleb went crashing into the forest by their house, pondering why he had married such a cantankerous hoddy-doddy; but after he'd walked a while, his fury faded and he couldn't remember what it was they had quarreled about. He could only remember that he loved her. He could only remember her dimples and her sweet ways, and what fragrant noodle pudding she made.

Instead of going straight back to put his arms around her and kiss her warm neck, he decided, since he was already there, to look in the forest for oak trees he could cut down later and take to the mill. He wandered farther in the woods, grew leg-weary, and, lying down to rest for just a moment, was overcome with all the greenness and slipped into a green sleep.

Before long the witch Yedida, who lived in a hidden cave in that forest, came shuffling by in her slippers, saying secret spells to herself. She stopped short where Caleb was lying, snoring away like a beehive. "How timely!" she snickered. "Here's my chance to test that new spell Cousin Iggdrazil just taught me."

Squatting down, she touched her skinny thumb to the tip of Caleb's left forefinger and, careful not to wake him, barely wheezed these words:

> "Ammy whammy,
> Ibbin bammy,
> This is now
> A bow-wow-wow."

And there at her feet, instead of a snoring carpenter, was a snoozing dog. "What a darling spell!" she crowed; and pleased to have worked her day's worth of mischief, the witch departed, swollen with pride.

It was sundown when Caleb woke. First he yawned, then he stretched, then he reached to scratch in his armpit. With his *leg*?! Holy gazoly! His eyes bulged and his big mouth hung open and slavered. Where he should have seen a belt and breeches and a pair of heavy brogans, he beheld the belly and hairy legs of a dog!

He was on his feet in an instant, all four of them. Terrified, he spun around to see what he could see of himself. He couldn't believe what he saw. Of course not! Such things don't happen. Oh no? "This is clearly me," he realized. "I'm not dreaming. I'm a dog!"

"*Now* what?" he wondered. "Well, all I can do is go back and explain what happened." And he began trotting homeward, stunned by his new condition, his tail swinging from side to side. Whatever in the world of wonders was it all about? He was suddenly a dog. True, but he was also Caleb the carpenter. He had Caleb's thoughts. And he was running home to his wife, Kate, wasn't he? Yes, on four legs, and sick at heart.

Night fell and there was a simple moon. Kate, at home, was stumbling from room to room, bumping into furniture, dizzy with dread. She had been at every window again and again, peering out, and had been outside many times, but had seen no part of Caleb.

Had her husband deserted her? she asked herself. No, he loved her; he had said so often. But maybe he was fed up with her. Or maybe something had happened to him, a catastrophe.

Caleb was outside the door just then, reluctant to come in and show himself. He was ashamed of being a dog. But at last he worked up the courage to scratch. When Kate held the door open and he saw her pale, worried face, he scrambled over the sill, thrust his hairy paws up on her apron, and strove to say, "Katie, it's me!" Only a suffering growl escaped his throat. He tried again. And again. He could imagine himself saying "Kate," but couldn't say it.

"Poor, lost animal!" she cried. She gave him some water in a bowl on the floor, and a piece of leftover ham. Caleb drank avidly, but he had no heart to eat. When Kate put a shawl on her shoulders and started to leave, he knew she was going out to look for him, and tried to stop her. He held her shoe in his teeth.

"Stand aside, silly dog," she scolded. "This is no time for games. I must find my dear husband. He may be in terrible trouble." Caleb let her go and trotted gravely after.

All night they traipsed through the moon-laced forest. There was no finding Caleb because there he was behind his wife, with the shape and the shadow of a dog.

At home again in the cool morning, her shoes wet with dew, weary Kate fell asleep in a chair Caleb had made for her, and the maker slept at her feet.

When they woke at noon, Kate searched again in the forest, with the woebegone Caleb dogging her heels, sniffing the ground for no good reason except that he felt he had to.

Then she went into town and made inquiries there, in the tavern, at the post office, in the shops, on the green. Everyone was deeply concerned and would keep an eye out, but no one had caught even a glimpse of Caleb—coming, going, or standing still.

When Kate went to bed that night, Caleb got into his rightful place beside her, snuggled against her dear body, kissed her sweet neck as he'd always done, and sighed out his sorrows. She welcomed the dog's warmth. With him there, she felt less bereft.

She fell asleep with her arm around him, but he was awake all night, wide-eyed, wondering. How could he manage to make himself known to his wife? If he could only tell her somehow that the dog in her arms was her husband! If he could only return to his natural state. Or if Kate could perhaps become a dog. Then they could be dogs together.

Kate decided to keep Caleb. She bought him a collar studded with brass, and she named him Rufus because his fur was reddish, like her husband's hair. She taught him tricks: to stand on two legs, to sit, to shake hands, to fetch things she asked for, to count by barking, to bow. She could hardly believe how fast he learned.

Whenever their friends came calling, Kate would show off her dog.
He enjoyed these gatherings, the human conversation, but he didn't like
to have his head patted by his old cronies.

Kate grew to love her dog, very much indeed. But, though they gave each other comfort, they were far from happy. Kate longed for her missing husband; she couldn't understand why he'd left her. And how Caleb wished he could speak and explain! He would sprawl by her feet, gnawing a bone, while she worked at her weaving. Often a tear would hang from her lashes, or she would stare through the window and sigh, and Caleb would put his paws in her lap and lick her sad face. Kate would scratch fondly behind his ears, caress his fur, and tell him how lucky she was to have such a faithful friend.

One afternoon in late summer, when Caleb was stretched under a tree reveling in the green smell of the grass, some other dogs turned up and enticed him into a romp. Caleb loved it, but soon quit and retired into the house, where the others dared not follow. He had discovered that being a dog among dogs could be joyous sport, but he didn't want to forget who he was.

The dogs came by a few times more, but Caleb gave them no encouragement, and they stopped coming.

Months passed, in their proper order. From time to time Caleb was drawn back to the place where he'd turned into a dog. He hoped he might find in that luckless spot some clue to the secret of his transformation. He would lie down where he had fallen asleep that day, pretend to be sleeping again, and watch intently through slitted eyes. Chipmunks scurried about in sudden darts, birds were busy in the branches, leaves bent with the roving breezes, a legion of insects hummed. Grasshoppers, on occasion, catapulted through the air. Caleb saw nothing extraordinary. He tried chewing various plants, on the wild chance that one of them might change him back to a man. No such thing even began to happen.

Winter came; snow fell. It was eight months since Caleb had become a dog. He kept warm near the glowing fireplace, dozing much of the day. He watched Kate move through the house, hopeless now about ever being able to reveal his true self. And what if she did learn who he was? Would it make her happier? Well, she would know that he hadn't deserted her; but would she relish having a dog for a husband? He decided she wouldn't.

One crisp, starry night, long after Christmas, burglars crept up to the warm, sleeping house. They deftly pried open a window and stole into the parlor with a drift of icy air. But Caleb was instantly up and barking. He scurried through the bedroom door straight at the intruders.

"Fry this stupid mongrel!" cried the shorter burglar, trying to fend him off. Caleb locked his jaws on the man's arm. The taller burglar seized Caleb by the collar, but Caleb held fast.

Kate, torn from her dreams by the hubbub, saw her brave dog fighting two men and ran to help. She pummeled the one who had hold of Caleb and pulled his coarse hair. He wheeled and flung her to the floor, hissing broken curses through his beard. That very instant Caleb rushed him, hoarsely snarling and showing his dangerous fangs. The terrified thief drew a knife from a pocket in his rags and slashed crazily at Caleb, slicing a bit of skin off a toe on his front paw.

A miracle! Caleb didn't yelp with pain. He yelled the word "Ouch!" and holding his injured paw to his mouth, he was astounded to find it a bleeding hand. The thief had cut the toe that had been the finger through which the witch Yedida had worked her spell, and the spell was undone! Caleb was Caleb again, clad in his old clothes.

"It's me!" he shouted exultantly. Kate gaped, then "Caleb!" she shrieked. The thieves, frightened to the point of insanity, dived through the window and vanished. They ran so fast they left no footprints in the snow.

Caleb and Kate leaped into each other's arms and cleaved together for a long time.

Much later, when they were able to talk intelligently, Caleb told her, or tried to tell her, what had happened—so far as he knew. What had actually happened they never found out. Like many another thing, it remained a mystery.

About the Author

William Steig (1907–2003) grew up in New York City in a family where artistic creativity was valued and allowed to flourish. His father, a housepainter by trade, and his mother, a seamstress, were both artists. So was his older brother, Irwin, who gave Steig his first painting lesson. The family did not have many books in the house, but they often went to the library, where Steig discovered many wonderful stories, including his favorite, Carlo Collodi's *Pinocchio*.

Steig drew his first cartoons for his high school newspaper, and after high school went on to study art at City College of New York and the National Academy of Design. When the stock market crash of 1929 left his father penniless, it was up to Steig to support his family, which he did as a freelance illustrator and cartoonist. In 1930, he sold his first cartoon to *The New Yorker*, and in 1933, for the first time, one of his illustrations appeared on the cover of that magazine. These early sales marked the beginning of a long and happy association with *The New Yorker*, where Steig's drawings soon became a popular fixture and remained so for eight decades.

In 1968, at the age of sixty-one, Steig embarked on a new and very different career with the publication of his first books for children, *C D B !* and *Roland the Minstrel Pig*. In 1970, his third children's book, *Sylvester and the Magic Pebble*, won the prestigious Caldecott Medal. Numerous books and awards followed, including *The Amazing Bone*, a Caldecott Honor Book, and *Abel's Island* and *Doctor De Soto*, both Newbery Honor Books. On the basis of his entire body of work, Steig was selected as the 1982 United States candidate for the Hans Christian Andersen Medal for Illustration and subsequently as the 1988 United States candidate for Writing.

In his 1970 acceptance speech for the Caldecott Medal, Steig said: "Art, including juvenile literature, has the power to make any spot on earth the living center of the universe; and unlike science, which often gives us the illusion of understanding things we really do not understand, it helps us to know life in a way that still keeps before us the mystery of things. It enhances the sense of wonder. And wonder is the respect for life."